C000104514

Wolf Kiss

Sarah Emambocus

Published by Sarah Emambocus, 2023.

This is a work of fiction. Similarities to real people, places, or events are entirely coincidental.

WOLF KISS

First edition. January 1, 2023.

ISBN: 979-8215602140

Written by Sarah Emambocus.

Table of Contents

Chapter 1

Have you ever wished to be someone amazing? Ever wondered if you could ever have a special power which only certain people have? I never imagined that one day I would ever be in this situation. Our story begins in the hospital where a young woman is giving birth as she cries saying, *"I can't do this!."* Ajax kisses her hand saying, *"Alizah my love you can do this!."* Alizah pushes and finally gives birth to a baby girl however she soon feels weak while holding her baby girl and says, *"Ajax promise me you will keep her safe."* Ajax replies, *"of course my love, we will protect her together."* Alizah kisses her daughter saying tearfully, *"my beautiful and brave little Anahita."* The baby opens its eyes revealing a sea-blue like colour as Alizah slowly closes her eyes. Ajax takes the baby and calls the doctor saying, *"HELP! HELP! MY WIFE NEEDS HELP!."* The doctor comes in and tries to resuscitate Alizah however he says, *"I'm sorry we couldn't save her".* Ajax cries tearfully while holding his daughter; a few days later Alizah is buried as Ajax looks after Anahita; however, one night a group of men ambush the house as Ajax escapes and takes Anahita to a nearby convent saying, *"I'm sorry baby girl... you will be safe here until the time comes...."* He places her on the doorstep and leaves a locket before knocking the door and running away. One of the sister bring Anahita inside as someone says, *"poor baby! We will look after her!."* Elsewhere a young baby boy is sleeping in a cot as his mother Sierra says, *"my little Matteo! One day you will be a strong Alpha and find your mate."* Sierra turns for a moment just as Matteo wakes up crying; Sierra cuddles her son in her arms and brings him over to the window as they look at the night sky filled with stars. Years pass as Anahita grows to five years old and her birthday is celebrated at the convent; Anahita's best friend Neirah says, *"happy birthday bestie!."* Anahita opens the present to see a small group of photos of them together; Anahita hugs Neirah saying, *"this is the best birthday gift ever!."* The sisters bring out the cake as the children sing, *'Happy birthday Anahita!.'* Anahita makes a wish before blowing out the candle; the cake is shared with all the kids as Anahita soon sits in her favourite spot the window in her room; Neirah comes asking, *"bestie, won't you come dance with me?."* Anahita gets up and smiles replying, *"ok."* She comes back downstairs and enjoys the party; Later that night it is a full moon as Anahita wakes up and heads into the nearby woods; she looks around wondering, *'why am I here?.'* She soon feels something happening inside her as she transforms into a white wolf; she looks around wondering, *'why is everything so small?.'* She runs to a nearby river and sees her reflection as the white wolf and thinks, *'is that me?.'* She looks at the moon and howls; Elsewhere Matteo is also in his wolf form as he runs around the wild forest; Matteo looks at the moon wondering, *'will I ever find mate?.'* Anahita soon changes back to her human form and comes back to her room quietly. The next few days are quiet as she wonders, *'should I tell Neirah? Will she believe me? what am I?.'* A few months later Anahita is able to control her ability and also research what being a wolf is. One evening Anahita sneaks out and heads into the forest as she changes into her wolf; Neirah sees Anahita's wolf form and asks, *"Anahita! W-what are you?."* Anahita turns back to her human form as Neirah backs away scared; Anahita says, *"I would never hurt you Neirah! You're my best friend!."* Neirah runs away as Anahita wonders, *'will she ever be able to forgive me?.'* Back in her room Neirah is stunned and doesn't know how to reach to finding out her best friend is a wolf; Neirah does some research on her laptop; Meanwhile Matteo is training in his wolf form and is very skilled. Matteo soon changes back to his human form as his dad Aztec says, *"son very soon when you grow up! you will be able to take over the academy!."* Matteo smiles happily while Anahita comes back to her room and sees Neirah asleep. A few days later Neirah avoids Anahita which makes her feel sad however soon Neirah comes to Anahita saying, *"we need to talk."* Anahita says, *"you can ask me anything Neirah!."* Neirah asks, *"how did you discover your wolf form? What are your powers? How do you change?."* Anahita replies, *"I only discovered recently that I am a white wolf... I don't know yet what powers I have, and I change if needed."* Later that night Neirah and Anahita come into the forest as Anahita changes into her wolf form; Neirah bends down and looks at her calling, *"Anahita! Bestie!."* The Wolf turns and places its paw on Neriah's lap in which Neirah says while stroking it, *"you would never hurt me! you are so soft and cuddly!."* The Wolf Howls before running into the wild; Ajax watches from a safe distance as he holds an envelope thinking, *'very soon you will be able to go to this place.'*

Chapter 2

Time flies by as Neirah and Anahita grow up; Neirah is fifteen while Anahita is sixteen; the sister comes in saying, *"Anahita as you know it's your sixteen's birthday which means that you will be moving out soon."* Neirah says, *"please don't let her go! she's my best friend!."* Sister Annabelle says, *"I am sorry but maybe this letter might be able to help you."* Anahita takes the letter as she touches her locket before opening the letter and reading it,

Dear Ms Anahita,

I am pleased to inform you that you have been accepted to Wolverton Academy in Alaska. Please accept our congratulations; this year, we received many excellent applications from talented individuals and only had the opportunity to admit a select few students. We feel you will be a great fit for our academy in which we would be delighted to offer you a scholarship. I look forward to hearing from you soon and seeing you on campus!

Your sincerely, Aztec

Anahita puts the letter down surprised as Neirah asks, *"what is it? what's wrong?."* Neirah takes the letter and reads it before saying, *"you got in! oh my god! This is fantastic!."* Neirah takes out her laptop and researches the Academy while Anahita looks out of the window at the sky wondering, *'could my future be at the Academy? Who sent my application in?.'* Neirah says, *"bestie come and have a look! the Academy is so prestigious... I can't believe you got in!."* Anahita says, *"I didn't apply for this! what If it's something* bad?." Neirah replies, *"now you're just being silly Anahita! This is a fantastic opportunity for you!."* Neirah has a look at the staff and sees a cute looking boy saying, *"he's lush! He would be perfect for you!."* Anahita sees Matteo's picture however rolls her eyes and says, *"come on let's get some lunch! I'm starving!."* Elsewhere at the Academy Matteo was outside training with his brother just as Aztec comes out saying, *"Matteo I need to talk to you!."* Matteo grabs his water bottle as Aztec says, *"you know what's been happening lately son? the attack.. danger!."* Matteo understands his father's worries and assures him that things will be ok soon. Later that evening Anahita sleeps however soon sees a vision in which a black wolf with red eyes comes near her; Anahita stirs in her sleep while meanwhile back in Alaska outside the academy Elliot says, *"Alpha Matteo, there's been another attack at the border."* Josh says, *"we're all in danger."* Matteo says, *"the girl will arrive soon.. when she does.. she's going to change everything. She's going to save us all!."* They all change into the Wolf form and run into the forest. Anahita soon wakes up and sees Neirah asleep as she sighs wondering, *'what was that dream about? who was that Wolf?.'* A few weeks later Neirah helps Anahita to pack as she says, *"I'm still not sure if I should go."* Neirah looks at Anahita saying, *"I know you're scared but this will be a fantastic opportunity for you! who know you may even find your mate?."* Anahita laughs asking, *"have you been reading Twilight and watching Wolf Movies and documentaries again?."* Neirah replies, *"maybe.. ok I have but it would be so amazing!."* Anahita brings down her suitcase and bags as she hugs the sisters thanking her for everything; Neirah comes to the train station with Anahita who hugs her asking, *"you won't forget me right?."* Anahita replies, *"you're my bestie and sister! I will never forget you.*" Anahita boards the train as Neirah waves goodbye; Anahita touches her locket wondering, *'what will life be like there?.'* She soon closes her eyes and takes a little rest; meanwhile Matteo is looking out at the sky wondering, *'is she really out there? the girl destined to save us?.'* Soon there is a knock on the door as Anahita wakes up to find someone handing her a tray of food of bottle of water; she says, *"thank you for this."* The person nods and leaves as Anahita puts it on the table and pours some of the water into a cup however as she touches it; it instantly becomes ice. Anahita wonders, *'what is this?.'* She again touches the water cup which melts the water back from an ice into liquid before thinking, *'this is weird. let's just eat and sleep... tomorrow will be a busy day.'* Anahita began to eat the food and drank the water before falling asleep; she had a strange dream that she was running through the woods and standing on ice as a gulf of flames were around her. Anahita saw a figure who tried to help her however the face was unclear; Anahita woke up startled and wondered, *'who was this guy? Why am I having such dreams?.'* Meanwhile Matteo was in his bed as he thought, *'I hope I find her tomorrow... I think my heart will intuitively know the girl..,'* he soon closes his eyes and drifts to bed as does Anahita.

Chapter 3

The next morning Anahita arrives at the station as her phone beeps; she sees a message from Neirah reading, *'hey are you at Wolverton Academy yet?.'* Anahita texts back, *'I've just stepped off the train!.'* Neirah texts back, *'I can't believe you actually got into the elite Wolfblood school; everyone who goes there is basically famous bestie!.'* Anahita looks around as she sees a cute looking guy and snaps his photo before sending it to Neirah who texts back, *'OMG it's Alpha Mason... he's the HOTTEST Alpha! You have to speak to him!.'* Anahita texts back, *'I'm too nervous....'* Neirah says, *'that's the WORST excuse ever bestie! You only have one chance to make a first big impression.. just make sure you're not in sweats like you always are....'* Anahita texts back, *'how do you know that?.'* Neirah texts back, *'because I'm your bestie, now go show those boarding school bitches that you're the HOTTEST wolf in school!.'* Anahita heads back on the train thinking, *'if I want to make a big impression, then I need to change.. now.'* as she opens her luggage and grabs a short polka dot dress with leather jacket and ankle boots; she brushes her golden hair and soon comes out. Everyone begins to notice her as one of the girls named Emma asks her friend, *"who's she?."* The other girl with red hair named Scarlet replies, *"whoever she is, I think she doesn't belong here!."* Matteo looks at Anahita as he comes closer saying, *"it's you, the one I've been waiting for."* Matteo comes closer as Anahita feels a crackle of heat cut through the cold misty air; he looks at her saying, *"I've imagined what you'd be like, but I never expected this."* Anahita looks at Matteo for a moment before asking, *"you were waiting for me?."* Matteo says, *"I'm amiably surprised... it's just-"*. Before he can say anything Josh screams, *"ALL STUDENT PLEASE BOARD THE BUS TO CAMPUS IMMEDIATELY!."* Anahita says, *"I should go..."* Matteo says, *"take a ride with me to campus...."* Anahita's gaze meets Matteo as she sees a fire burning in his eyes; he says, *"there are things I need to tell you, Anahita. Things I need to show you..."* Scarlet comes over saying, *"if you don't take the ride, then I will newbie."* Anahita looks around replying, *"it's ok, I'll walk to campus."* Matteo says, *"be careful out there, Anahita."* Scarlett takes Matteo's hand as they get into his sled which rides off; Anahita looks around at the empty station before grabbing her bag and begins to walk down the road before cutting into the forest in which she sees a sign *'Wolverton Academy- 3 Miles'.* She stops for a moment thinking, *'ugh I really wish I took that ride with Matteo.. I missed the bus....'* Just then a crack sound spooks Anahita as she looks around asking, *"h-hello? Hello? Is anyone there?."* The bushes begin to rattle as a brown wolf emerges as Anahita asks, *"hey little guy! Are you lost?."* The wolf growls angrily at her as Anahita is frightened and screams, *"AAAAAAAAAAAH!."* Meanwhile Matteo brings Scarlet to the campus as she says, *"Matteo maybe you could show me around?."* Matteo immediately leaves as Anahita is still scared and slowly backs away; the wolf gnarls at her; just then a black wolf emerges and fights the brown wolf who soon runs off; the wolf changes back as Anahita says, *"Matteo.. t-thanks for saving me... how did you get here so fast?."* Matteo comes closer replying, *"I knew you'd be out here alone, and I sensed you were in trouble."* Anahita says confused, *"you* sensed me?." Matteo replies, *"it's hard to explain, it's like I felt-"*. Matteo comes closer and reaches to touch Anahita's arm; Anahita soon feels a soft halo light glow from where Matteo touches her; she moves back in surprise asking, *"w-what happened? w-what was that?."* Matteo replies, *"that glow is the reason you've been brought here, Anahita. Let me touch you again and I'll show you why."* Matteo comes closer towards Anahita as a spark of electricity lights up the small space between their bodies; Matteo says, *"I could tell you, but I'd rather show you.. let me touch you for real Anahita."* Anahita took a deep breath before replying, *"Matteo...o ok.. touch me."* Matteo smiles as he gently moves closer taking his face and stroking her face lightly; the light brightens with his touch and suddenly Anahita feels her whole body filled with a pleasant warmth. Matteo says, *"I didn't think it would really happen, but... look at you..."* Anahita looks at Matteo asking, *"Matteo, what is this?."* He replies, *"can't you feel it, Anahita? It's fate, it means we were meant to find each other."* Anahita asks, *"but...how? I barely know you?."* Matteo says, *"I'll explain everything, just... not here."* Anahita nods as he takes her luggage, and they soon head to Wolverton Academy. Soon inside Anahita says, *"Matteo you need to tell me what happened out there! what happened in the forest? What was that glow?."* Matteo replies, *"you have so many questions? You really don't realise what this means? How special you are?."* Anahita says, *"special? I don't feel really special.. I mean you hardly know me.. what's going on?."* Matteo takes her hand saying, *"this is why you're here, when we touched I thought it was true but now I know for sure. Anahita,,, you're my mate."* Anahita is shocked just as a golden light engulfs around them.

Chapter 4

Anahita looks at Matteo who is smiling saying, *"Anahita you're my mate."* Anahita wonders, *'am I dreaming right now? his mate? Could I be Matteo's mate?.'* Matteo asks, *"what's wrong Anahita? What are you thinking about?."* He comes closer as he takes Anahita's hand and his gaze burns into her like fire. Anahita thinks, *'damn... I can feel the flame of desire between us.'* Matteo says, *"you and I are bound for life."* Anahita looks at him asking, *"this is a joke, right? That's impossible Matteo!."* Matteo replies, *"it's not a joke Anahita, it's destiny! You're the mate of a powerful Alpha and you're a target now, we need to keep our bond a secret, atleast for now."* Anahita looked into Matteo's eyes and saw sincerity thinking, *'he's not lying or making anything up.'* Anahita asks, *"so what do we do now?."* Matteo replies, *"there's one way which I know we can be together, as wolves... we can transform now."* Anahita asks, *"what do you mean? what will transforming into our wolf form do?."* Matteo replies, *"transforming together will only strengthen our bond."* Anahita blushes as Matteo comes closer, his eyes filled with passion as he smiles saying in her ears, *"it'll bring us closer than ever."* Anahita smiles saying, *"ok let's do it then."* He brings her outside to a secret place in the woods as he says, *"ok now just imagine yourself as a wolf, and then you'll transform.. the colour of your wolf symbolises what power you have in wolf form."* Anahita nods as she takes a deep breath, closes her eyes, and transforms into her wolf form which is white with a little shade of artic blue; Anahita wonders, *'what could my powers be?.'* Matteo says, *"you look as beautiful as the first snowfall.. your powers are speed and beauty."* Matteo changes into his wolf form as the black wolf with brown eyes as Anahita looks at him wondering, *'why does it he look so familiar? This is the first time I am seeing him... wait a second.. it's him the one from my dream..'* Matteo mind-links Anahita asking, *"can you hear me, Anahita?."* Anahita replies, *"yes I can, but how?."* Matteo says, *"because you're my mate Anahita, our minds are connected in wolf form."* Anahita teases Matteo saying, *"you must try this with all the girls, Mr Flirty!."* Matteo says, *"no! I've never been able to feel anything for other girls but with you... there's a connection."* Anahita says, *"race you Matteo!!."* Matteo says, *"you're on but there's no way you'll win!."* Anahita runs as Matteo follows behind her as they roam around the woods eventually coming to a secret rooftop; they change back into human form as Anahita sees the northern lights shining in the sky; she smiles happily saying, *"wow this place is amazing!."* Matteo says, *"it feels so good finally to be able to share this with my mate."* Matteo wraps his arms around Anahita in a gentle but sure embrace. Anahita wonders, *'what is this warm feeling I am getting in my stomach? I can feel butterflies....'* Matteo still holding her says, *"it's you, you're the one I've been waiting for."* He soon lets her go as she turns to look at him asking, *"how did I get this lucky? Hold me tighter... it just feels so natural."* Matteo takes her hand replying, *"you're the one I want... I'll do whatever it takes to prove it to you Anahita.. do you realise how special and remarkable you are? Wolves don't reach their full power potential until they find a mate."* Anahita smiles at him as they still hold hands; he says, *"who knows what other powers you may hold but whatever it is, it will only grow.. as long as our bond gets stronger.*" Matteo brings her closer as Anahita feels the sparks and feelings grow between them; he says, "*we can do it now, commit to each other fully. We'll do a private ceremony as wolves.*" Anahita smiles saying, "*let's do this Matteo!.*" They change back into their wolf form and sit on the rail as Matteo says, "*Anahita, as your mate this is my vow I will always protect you, support you and care for you. I promise to honour this bond from now until the end of time.*" Anahita says, "*I promise you Matteo that I will respect you, trust you and forever be loyal to you.*" Matteo says, "*I will always trust you, Anahita...*" They come closer as white light shines between them as Matteo says, "*I promise to honour this bond from now and until the end of time.*" The light soon fades as Matteo nuzzles Anahita's face against his own; Anahita thinks, '*wow we made a promise of eternal love... I hope that me and Matteo forever stay happy.*' They soon leave and head back to the Academy; they change back into their human form as Matteo kisses Anahita's hand saying, "*good night my love!.*" Anahita blushes as she heads down the corridor however soon feels something and turns saying, "*hello? Is someone there?.*" She turns to see a dark shadow and thinks, '*I need to walk faster!.*' She runs upstairs and soon gets into bed. The next morning Anahita wakes up as she sees a young girl in her room saying, "*good morning, Anahita! I'm Vesta your roomie.*" Anahita smiles saying, "*it's nice to meet you.*" Vesta says, "*hey! you're not in purple, I guess you haven't found your mate yet?.*" Anahita says annoyed, "*excuse me?.*"

Chapter 5

Vesta sees Anahita's annoyed expression replying, *"chill out Anahita! Wearing purple is how we show other wolves we're mated here.. I mated with Josh last year. You literally can't wear purple if you're single it's a magic thing."* Just then Scarlet comes in with her two friends saying, *"for sure someone like you would never be able to wear purple! Who would be dumb enough to mate with you?."* Anahita turns around replying, *"excuse me? why don't you mind your own business?."* Vesta says, *"yeah, it's pretty bizarre of you to spy on people in their rooms."* Scarlet says fuming, *"shut up, Vesta!."* They soon leave as Vesta says annoyed, *"ugh she's such a she-devil! If you wear purple, it'll drive her mad that you have a mate, and she doesn't."* Anahita remembers Matteo and their moment last night as she opens the wardrobe and wears a purple blouse; Vesta asks, *"have you really got a mate? Wow Scarlet is going to be so jealous!."* Anahita freshens up and they soon into the main hall after breakfast as Scarlet scowls seeing Anahita in purple wondering, *'who could be her mate?.'* Matteo waves out to Anahita who comes over; he says, *"I hope you got settled in okay last night, you look cute in your blouse."* Anahita smiles and then wonders, *'should I tell Matteo about last night?.'* Matteo senses something is bothering Anahita asking, *"what's wrong, Anahita?."* Anahita takes a deep breath before replying, *"actually Matteo, someone followed me to my room."* Matteo says, *"this cannot be happening! If they hurt you, I swear...."* Anahita says, *"it was probably nothing... maybe it was a prank."* Matteo says, *"you can't assume that Anahita, Elliot's supposed to be watching the border. We've had rogue wolves trying to cross the border for weeks. I need to make sure Elliot doesn't allow them to succeed."* Matteo leaves as Josh comes to Anahita saying, *"Elliot's Matteo Beta which means right hand man and my brother unfortunately... I'm Josh by the way...."* Anahita says, *"it's nice to meet you."* Josh says, *"Elliot's always been jealous of Matteo."* Vesta comes over as Josh smiles at her and they leave; Anahita looks around at the other students just as a girl comes over to her asking, *"hi, excuse me are you Anahita Saunders?."* Anahita replies, *"yeah, what's up?."* The girl says, *"this is for you."* She hands her a piece of paper before leaving as Anahita opens it and reads the message, *'report to the office ASAP!.'* Anahita looks around wondering, *'who could have sent me this? am I in trouble?.'* Anahita comes into the office saying, *"hello? Anybody there?"* just then Elliot pushes her saying, *"the name's Elliot... nice to meet you, Anahita!."* Elliot comes closer to Anahita and wraps a rope around her arms as she struggles to free herself, Elliot only tightens his grip. She asks irritated, *"what the hell do you think you are doing?! Get your hands off me!."* Elliot replies, *"sorry no can do.. I need you."* Anahita says, *"you're supposed to be guarding the border!."* Elliot says, *"I'm done being Matteo's lap dog. He doesn't deserve the Alpha title; I do and you're going to help me take it from him!."* Anahita calls out, *"Matteo?! Matteo!!!."* Elliot says, *"he can't help you now, sweetheart! You think you're so special, don't you?."* Elliot made Anahita face him as she glared angrily at him he taunted her saying, *"you think you're the Alpha's favourite?."* Anahita replies, *"what, are you jealous Elliot?."* Elliot angrily says, *"why the hell would I be jealous? You're nothing!."* Elliot comes closer as his facial expression soon turns into a twisted evil grin; he leans in closer as his slimy face is inches away from Anahita who wonders, *'damn is this guy seriously trying to kiss me?!.'* Elliot says, *"Matteo wants you... but I'm going to make you mine sweetheart!."* Anahita soon sees someone from the corner of her eye sneaking in; she thinks, *'it's Matteo! He can't catch me kissing his Beta!.'* Anahita stomps on Elliot's foot before pushing him away; Matteo asks, *"what the hell is going on here?!."* Matteo frees Anahita who then slaps Elliot saying, *"that's for trying to kiss me you asshole!."* Elliot says, *"she clearly wanted the Beta, not the Alpha, sorry bro!."* Anahita glares coldly at Elliot as Matteo says angrily, *"some Beta you are... trying to force yourself on innocent students when you should be doing your JOB!."* Elliot angrily growls saying, *"AAARGH!."* Matteo says, *"you've gone way too far this time, Elliot!."* He grabs a knife as Elliot asks, *"oh yeah? So, what are you going to do about it, Alpha boy?."* Matteo replies, *"I'm going to kill you!."* Anahita was shocked by Matteo's word as she watched Elliot and Matteo about to fight.

Chapter 6

Anahita watches Elliot and Matteo fight as Matteo says, *"you've hurt Anahita, Elliot.. and now it's time to pay!."* He grabs the knife and wounds Elliot before trying to attack again however Anahita says, *"Matteo, please stop! don't do it! he's your Beta!."* Matteo turns to Anahita and hesitates while looking at her replying coldly, *"not anymore."* Elliot leaves but not before saying, *"you'll regret this, both of you!."* Matteo drops the knife as he says, *"I'm so sorry, Anahita, I'm never leaving you again."* He moves closer to Anahita as she feels his breath on her cheek, and she soon feels a soft glow dance before her eyes. Anahita says, *"Matteo, there is it again... that glow."* Matteo says, *"the closer we get, the stronger it becomes Anahita. You know what would happen if we kissed right now?."* Anahita replies, *"what?."* Matteo says, *"something completely magical, if our lips touched, I bet we would light up the world."* Anahita giggles before pulling Matteo closer for a kiss; as their lips meet an intense warmth blossoms in Anahita's stomach as she wonders, *'wow Matteo was right.. this kiss feels magical...'* A halo of light as golden as the sun glows from beneath Anahita's skin making her tingle. Matteo stops as he asks smiling, *"did you feel that Anahita?."* She smiles replying, *"the warmth.. it's like nothing I've ever felt before."* Matteo says, *"that Anahita... that's fate! we were meant to find each other, we were meant to be in this moment."* Just then Aztec comes in saying, *"rogues are at the border, closer than ever."* Matteo says, *"dad, I'm dealing with it."* Aztec says, *"these wolves don't care that you're the Alpha, Matteo, they want to create anarchy... they want to destroy everything this academy stands for."* He sees Anahita asks, *"I'm sorry... who are you?."* Anahita replies, *"I'm a friend of your son's."* Matteo says, *"she's a new friend, Anahita."* Aztec says, *"this conversation is for the inner circle only, **OUT!**."* Anahita nods and heads out to the door as Aztec tells Matteo, *"the rogues have a secret weapon, Matteo, they've got an Elemental on their side, a wolf capable of controlling and creating fire. Fire that could burn down our academy in seconds, it's only a matter of time before they breach the border."* The next day in class Mr Saxon says, *"today we are going to practise chemical reactions, pair up with your partners and get to work."* Josh says, *"so...Matteo told me what went down between you and Elliot."* Anahita asks, *"why would he tell you?."* Josh replies, *"I'm his new Beta."* Anahita says, *"but your brother almost killed me and Matteo!."* Josh says, *"let me make one thing clear, I'm not my brother and I'm not the one you need to worry about, not when a fire Elemental is about to storm the academy."* Anahita asks, *"what exactly is an Elemental?."* Josh says, *"oh right, you're new here! they're rare and incredibly dangerous, there are only four wolves in the world who can control the elements, these are Fire, Water, Wind and Earth.. if this fire Elemental lights up our academy... we'll all burn!."* Just then there is an explosion as Scarlett gloats while Anahita says annoyed, *"SCARLET!!."* Mr Saxon comes back and holds a green powder in his hand saying, *"fireflower? This is an extremely explosive and dangerous herb!! Tell me who did this, or I'll report you to Alpha Matteo! You'll be mopping the dungeons in detention for a week."* Scarlett says, *"and you can say goodbye to being teacher's pet! Matteo was never into bad girls!."* Anahita thinks, *'Scarlet really thinks she can* *embarrass me and ruin my relationship with Matteo....'* Anahita says, *"Mr Saxon, Scarlet was responsible for this!."* Scarlet says, *"she's obviously lying, I'm the top student in the class!."* Anahita shows proof in Scarlet's hand to Mr Saxon saying, *"I'm not lying, see?."* Mr Saxon angrily says, *"Scarlet! You know fireflower is banned on this campus! You'll be reported at once! I hope you're ready for a week's detention young lady!."* Scarlet scowls angrily saying, *"I'll get you back for this!."* Anahita says, *"whatever, Scarlet!."* Josh laughs as Scarlet leaves with Mr Saxon. Soon outside the office Matteo says, *"this is really disappointing, Scarlet."* Scarlet says, *"but-".* Matteo says, *"you know we have a zero-tolerance policy for this behaviour, next time you're out!."* Scarlet leaves as Matteo soon sees Anahita; he comes over saying, *"everyone's talking about what a badass you were in class!."* Anahita asks, *"really?."* Matteo replies, *"yep I know you were tough but standing up to Scarlet... wow!."* Anahita feels Matteo's fingers trace up her arm as his mouth quirks up in a flirty smile. He says, *"you're even braver than I thought."* Just as they are about to share a kiss; Josh comes over saying, *"come to the border, NOW!."* They all run out and see the flames as Matteo tells Josh, *"get all the students in their dorms, GO!."* Josh runs as Matteo turns to Anahita says, *"this is Elemental fire, it'll burn everything in its path and it's about to reach the stable."* Matteo runs and grabs a bucket of water and throws it on the flames however the flames hiss and then rise even higher into the sky. Anahita says, *"it's getting worse!."* Matteo says, *"the fire is too strong! You shouldn't be here, Anahita! It's too dangerous."* Anahita says, *"Matteo, no! I'm not helpless, we're in this together! I won't let you get hurt."* Matteo says, *"but it's my job to protect you."* He jumps in the stable as the fire spreads as Anahita coughs however suddenly a voice breaks through the dense smoke clouding her mind. The voice says, *'Anahita, you know what you have to do.'*

Chapter 7

Anahita holds out her hand in which she feels a pulsing sensation beneath her skin; a small blue energy comes out of her hand as Matteo says shocked, *"what are you...?."* She throws the blue energy from her hands towards the fire, water rushes from Anahita's palms onto the flames. Anahita says shocked, *"what the hell..? what did I just do...?."* Matteo says, *"keep going! Whatever you're doing is working! I'm going to get the horses out of the stables!."* Anahita worriedly says, *"MATTEO! NO!."* Matteo jumps across the flames into the stable as Anahita's arms start to shake, a white heat rips through her veins. Anahita says scared, *"the fire, it's... fighting back?."* Matteo says, *"Anahita I believe in you! you can do this!."* Anahita takes a deep breath and closes her eyes thinking, *'I'm fighting to protect my mate and to show what I'm capable of.'* As she opens her eyes a large blue water energy emerges from her hand as she puts out the fire; Matteo comes over to her saying, *"do you know how special you are?."* He pulls her into a big hug and they both fall on the ground; he says, *"you did it, Anahita!."* Anahita blushes and pulls Matteo closer as she feels the warmth of his body as he falls into her. They share a warm kiss as she wonders, *'every breath he takes is filled with his soft, spicy scent... damn I feel his lips on mine... his soft hair is between my fingers... when did I become so romantic?.'* Matteo says, *"I'm glad you're ok."* Anahita says, *"I'm so glad that we're both ok."* Matteo helps Anahita up as she asks, *"but how did I...? Matteo,* what the hell just happened?!." Matteo replies, "Anahita, what you just did... that was water magic. When were you going to tell me you're an Elemental?." Anahita answers, "how can I be one of the four Elementals?." Matteo says, "Elemental power is usually passed through bloodline... how could you not know? Anahita, how could you keep this from me?!." Anahita says, "I didn't keep anything from you!." Matteo says, "I hope that's true, the power you have is dangerous, Anahita. An Elemental nearly burned down the academy." Anahita says, "Matteo, I put the fire out!." Matteo says, "yes, you used your power to save me, that gives me hope for us but still...I can't help but question whether this whole mate thing was a mistake." Anahita looked hurt saying, "you're being unfair! give me a chance to prove it's not." Matteo comes closer and says, "I want to, Anahita, believe me but I also need to protect this academy. I can't call you my mate if I don't fully trust you." Anahita asks, "then how do I earn your trust, Matteo?." Matteo replies, "train with me, learn to use your power to fight by my side the rogues have an Elemental on their side, but we could too. You'd be our secret weapon." Anahita looks into Matteo's eyes as she sees a glimmer of hope begin to shine; Anahita nods as Matteo says, "go and get ready, we'll start training tonight." Later Anahita is doing her hair when Scarlet says, "the gym just closed, sweetie so if you were hoping to flex those muscles for Matteo, it'll have to wait." Anahita rolls her eyes saying, "actually I'm not that desperate but I guess you are." Scarlet says, "well atleast I'm not dressed like a literal slug, come on girls we have actual things to get back to." Anahita looks in the mirror wondering, 'Scarlet's right.. if I want to earn Matteo's trust I need to look like I'm serious about training.' She changes her outfit to something cute and practical; soon in the corridor Lexis says, "I bet Anahita will get shipped *back to her old home soon....*" Emma says, "*and then you'll finally get your moment with Matteo.*" Scarlet says, "*if he spends more time with me, I'm sure we'd become mates... our fathers always wanted us to get together, you know that why I'm taking these right now.*" Anahita sees a bouquet of lilies as Scarlet tells her friends, "*I know they are Matteo's favourite, a rare flower that only grows in my parent's garden.*" Anahita thinks, '*there's no way I'm letting Scarlett think she has a chance with Matteo... I bet I could control the water that's inside that vase....*' Anahita closes her eyes imagining herself holding the water that's in the vase; she raises her arms willing the water to leap from the vase; Scarlet drops the bouquet as she says, "*aargh! What the hell is your problem, Emma?!.*" Emma says, "*it... it wasn't me.*" Lexis says, "*it looked like...like magic.*" Scarlet says, "*UGH, now you've ruined my gift to Matteo.*" They leave as Anahita comes and picks up the lilies and heads over to meet Matteo outside by the pool; Matteo is surprised saying, "*Anahita, you brought my favourite flowers... how did you know?.*" Anahita replies, "*I'll never tell.*" Matteo says, "*mysterious, I like it, thank you. they are beautiful.*" Matteo smiles a warm grin that makes Anahita blush. Matteo says, "*Josh and my dad are preparing for another attack any day now, they think the border fire was just the beginning.*" Anahita soon notices Matteo's face filled with worry as she holds out her hand in which he takes it. Matteo says, "*thanks for being there for me, Anahita this means that understanding your power is more important than ever.*" Anahita asks, "*where do we start?.*"

Chapter 8

Matteo replies, *"with this."* He starts a fire as he says, *"imagine I'm your enemy, storming the gates of the academy. how do you use the water to get to me?."* Anahita says, *"I will cut a path through the fire."* She uses her power to douse the fire however Matteo says, *"not quite strong enough, but it's a good start. Elementals harness their power by tapping into one of two things: purpose or passion. How you're making, a difference or who you're doing it for.. you did this once already when you saved the stables... so I know you can do it again."* Anahita closes her eyes, raises her hands towards the water and says, *"I'll move this water with the force of my passion."* She thinks, *'I need to save this academy, I can't let this Elemental hurt anyone else.'* Anahita raises her hands, but the water barely moves from the pool; Matteo says, *"it's not personal enough maybe something is stopping you."* Matteo has an idea saying, *"let's try this instead."* Anahita looks at Matteo who soon pushes her into the water as she says shocked, *"what the hell?!."* He jumps into the pool saying, *"I need you to feel the water, Anahita, feel it and remember whose side you're fighting on."* Anahita closes her eyes and dives deep below as Matteo swims closer to her and takes her hand; she opens her eyes and they both share a moment. They go above as a small glows comes from Anahita's hand as she smiles while Matteo says, *"see? It's working, as my trust in you grows so does your power."* Anahita soon lets herself sink beneath the surface again as Matteo swims closer to her, his face inches from hers. Anahita thinks, *'he's coming closer...? why is my heartbeat racing so fast?.'* Matteo's lips moves towards Anahita as the buzz of power grows stronger; they share a passionate kiss underwater as the glow around grows deeper and brighter. She thinks, *'I want to be strong and to do what no one else can.. I can do this!.'* Anahita opens her eyes and lets out a small water ball which pushes Matteo aside; Anahita swims over saying, *"I'm sorry Matteo, are you ok?."* Matteo replies, *"I'm fine Anahita, you did great! Just remember I'm pushing you because I believe in us."* They both come out of the pool and dry off just when they hear a thunderstorm outside; in the forest the Wolves begin to run wild; Matteo says, *"the rogues.. Anahita they are here."* They run down the corridor and soon come into the office where Josh says, *"Matteo, I was just patrolling and the rogues... they are marching toward the border right now, a handful of them including the fire Elemental, they'll reach the academy by dawn."* Matteo says, *"Josh, you go and keep tracking them."* Josh leaves as Matteo turns to Anahita saying, *"this is it, the battle we knew was coming."* Anahita asks, *"do you think we can win Matteo?."* Matteo replies, *"I think we can try Anahita but with you on the battlefield, I know we'll succeed... I trust you and I need you Anahita."* Matteo pulls Anahita closer as he takes her in his arms, and she can feel his heart racing against her chest. Matteo's grips Anahita's waist and looks down at you his expression fierce and determined; Anahita thinks, *'this look of his alone sends a wave of heat coursing through my body.'* Matteo says, *"if I have you by my side... there's no way we won't defeat this Elemental."* Anahita says, *"of course, I'll fight with you!."* Matteo kisses her warmly as they fall into each other, the tension of the moment melts away. Matteo shoves Anahita against the wall pressing his body to hers saying, *"you're everything I've ever wanted, it's cruel that we can't just be together."* Anahita says, *"we are together."* Matteo says, *"so we need to make the most of it."* Matteo pulls Anahita into him as they share a kiss which deepens as she kisses his neck; he moans her name lovingly; a hungry growl escapes Anahita's lips as Matteo deepens the kiss. They soon stop as Matteo says, *"I wish this could last forever, but I have a job to do, I have to make sure the students are safely in hiding. I knew I could count on you to fight with me, so I got you this, it'll help tap into your powers... meet me at the border in an hour, I hope you'll be wearing it."* An hour later Aztec says, *"what is that girl doing here?."* Matteo says, *"dad, it's Anahita."* Matteo looks at Anahita and there is a wild determination burning in his eyes. Matteo says, *"she's going to be the reason we survive this fight."* Aztec asks, *"but what skills does she have?."* Matteo turns to Anahita says, *"go ahead, Anahita... it's time to show him!."* Anahita thinks, *'I'll use my power to dump water over his head!.'* A few moments late on the ice; Anahita closes her eyes before using the power to pour water on Aztec who is stunned saying, *"what the-?."* Josh comes there saying, *"oh my god, Anahita's-."* Aztec says, *"an Elemental!."* Aztec says, *"she can't be trusted, Matteo!."* Matteo says, *"she's only ever used her power for good."* Aztec says, *"I'll believe it when I see it."* Just then they are surrounded by Wolves as Anahita says, *"MATTEO!."* Josh says, *"they are here!."* Matteo says, *"you can do this, Anahita! I'm here for backup if you need me."* Matteo, Josh, and Aztec transform into Wolves and start fighting off the other Wolves. Blaze puts a ring of fire around Anahita surrounding her as she uses her power to douse it. Blaze says angrily, *"WHAT THE FUCK?! you're.... an Elemental?."*

Chapter 9

Anahita says, *"yeah, I guess you're not that special after all".*
Blaze says, *"clever... but what about this?".* He shoots the fireball at Anahita who ducks as Blaze says, "you're wasting your time! You're outnumbered, and your soldiers are weak". Blaze flicks his hand and sends a flame flying at Wolf Josh. Matteo screams, *"JOSH, NO!".* Anahita uses her power saying, *"I've got this, Matteo!".* However, as she steps forward she feels a scorch at her ankles and screams, *"OWWW!".* She looks down to find cuffs of fire encasing her legs as she falls to the ground. Blaze says, *"you're not going anywhere".* Blaze fires up on Josh again as he lets out an agonising howl and falls to the ground. Anahita watches sadly as Matteo rushes over as he transforms back into his human form as does Josh who is injured. Matteo says, *"you need to break free, Anahita! Think of me and remember where you get your power!."* Anahita gets up, closes her eyes, and invokes the image of Matteo in her mind; she sees him holding her close and soon breaks free from the flame around her. Blaze says, *"you're a pain in my ass, you know that? but I have a surprise of my own up my sleeve, he should be arriving any second and then you and your little boyfriend will die."* Anahita says, *"Matteo, there's someone else coming!."* Matteo rushes over as he says, *"I don't know much longer we can hold them; I don't know if we're ready for what's coming next".* Matteo squeezes Anahita's hand as his eyes darken with fear and passion. Matteo says, *"I'll do whatever it takes to protect*

us". Anahita says, *"Matteo, no!."* She takes his hand and create a water shield around them; A familiar voice says, *"this has been fun and all, but I've got an academy to destroy!."* Anahita recognises the voice as Matteo says, *"Elliot?!".* Elliot comes closer asking, *"did you miss me?!."* Anahita looks shocked as he says with a smirk, *"hello again, Anahita!."* Anahita looks in fear as the shield breaks around her and Matteo; a few moments later Matteo says, *"Anahita, take my hand".* She opens her eyes, takes Matteo's hand, and gets up. Elliot says, *"you two just don't give up, do you? you won't leave his side, even if it kills you".* Anahita says, *"you wish you had what we have! I'll never leave Matteo!".* Matteo's eyes light up with pride saying, *"I'll never leave hers".* Elliot says, *"then I guess I'll have to force you apart".* Matteo says, *"over my dead body!".* Elliot smirks saying, *"gladly".* Elliot lunges towards Anahita and Matteo as his face changed into a deadly grimace; Anahita spits and kicks him as Elliot stumbles backward. Matteo says, *"we aren't as weak as you think, Elliot!".* Elliot says, *"you may not be weak, but your students are".* Elliot leers at Matteo saying, *"I know where they are hiding...if I kill them will that shut you up?".* Elliot smirks before leaving as Matteo yells, *"NO!".* Aztec says, *"Go! we'll deal with Blaze!".* Anahita and Matteo run in as he says, *"Elliot hasn't gotten in yet! Come on, I know another way down".* They go through a shortcut as the students are crowded in fear and worry. Vesta says, *"Elliot's going to break down the door!".* Scarlet asks, *"is Anahita the one protecting us? Then we're all going to die!!".* Anahita gets annoyed saying, *"go out alone, then!".* Scarlett replies, *"I...can't, I don't know how to fight!".* Matteo says, *"Anahita does, and she will protect you all!".* Matteo looks at Anahita saying, *"we can't fight off all the rogues unless you use your power to shield us".* Just then there is a big bang from the door as Elliot comes with two Wolves beside him. Elliot yells, *"YOU'RE ALL DEAD!"*. He changes into his wolf form and is about to charge as Anahita uses her power to shield everyone; The two wolves soon run as Elliot scowls angrily saying, *"YOU THINK YOU ARE SO POWERFUL?!"*. Elliot tries to hurt Anahita making Matteo angry as he pushes Elliot aside; Elliot smirks saying, *"I will come back and destroy your mate!"*. Matteo angrily clenches his fist and goes after Elliot in the corridor; he grabs a knife as Elliot asks, *"you'd really murder your former Beta? Your brother? You think you're so much better than me... but you'd do anything to keep your power"*. Anahita comes out as she says, *"Matteo! Don't listen to him! you don't have to do this! that's not who you are, Matteo"*. Matteo says, *"as much as it kills me, I can't let him get away again"*. Anahita says, *"I know, Matteo..."*. Matteo says, *"no, you don't understand, Anahita! If I do this, I will never be the same"*. Elliot says, *"killing your own Beta leaves a scar... pain like you can't even imagine"*. As Matteo raises the knife, his face twists in anguish; Anahita feels the pain in her chest wondering, *'I have no choice... I won't let Matteo be scarred'*.

Chapter 10

Anahita says, *"give me the knife, Matteo!."* She takes the knife as Matteo says, *"Anahita, it's ok."* Anahita says, *"no, you don't always have to be strong, Matteo, let me do it this time."* Elliot says, *"no!! you cannot do this to me!."* Anahita says, *"who's a 'weak little girl' now?."* Anahita says, *"it's over, Elliot!."* Anahita plunges the knife into Elliot's chest as he soon falls to the ground and bleeds out. Anahita turns and hugs Matteo as he says, *"you saw how much that would hurt me... so you took on that pain instead, you don't know how much that means to me, Anahita."* Matteo kisses Anahita warmly as they soon head out to see many Wolves are dead; Aztec says, *"Blaze is dead."* Anahita sees Josh asking, *"how are you feeling, Josh?."* Josh replies, *"still sore but I'll get better."* Aztec says, *"Blaze was weakened thanks to Anahita's attacks."* Josh says, *"the students are ok, a little shaken up but they survived the rogue's attacks thanks to Anahita."* Matteo says, *"Elliot's dead too."* Josh says, *"then we burn the bodies, move on!."* Later Matteo and Anahita are talking nearby in the woods as he says, *"pretty eventful first week of college, huh? It feels like ever since I found you... my mate.. we've hardly had anytime to just be together... to get to know each other."* Anahita says, *"I feel like I already know you... I'm more interested in touching each other...sorry if that sounded a little weird."* Matteo blushes asking, *"oh yeah? Then what's my love language?."* Anahita replies, *"um.... physical touch?."* Matteo comes closer saying, *"I guess someone's* been paying attention, you wanna know the best way to really get to know each other?." Anahita asks, "what's that?." Matteo pulls Anahita closer as she feels him close gripping her hips in his hands and leaving behind trails of kisses up her neck. Anahita giggles as Matteo says, "since we're both such a big fan of physical touch... how about I touch every inch of your body?." Matteo leans in close, his voice barely a whisper against her cheek; his eyes dark and hungry as they drift down to her hip. Anahita wonders, 'damn I'm feeling like electric shocks all over my body...?.' Matteo says, "kiss me, Anahita!." Anahita nods as she kisses Matteo who pushes her against the tree as their kiss deepens with sparks; Anahita wraps her legs around Matteo who soon kisses her neck as she lets out a moan. Matteo says, "I love hearing you like that!." Anahita kisses Matteo passionately as she nibbles on his ears as he stops and looks at her for a moment before saying, "I'll have to punish you for that!." Anahita blushes and they continue to be intimate in gently removing each other's clothes. As the evening falls they are soon interrupted by Josh screaming, "ANAHITA! MATTEO! COME QUICKLY!." They both get change and rush over as Matteo asks, "what's wrong?." Josh replies, "it's Blaze, he's....gone." Aztec says, "but he left something behind." Aztec hands Matteo a piece of paper while Anahita asks, "what is it? what does it say?." Matteo replies, "it's for you, Anahita! It's addressed to you." Anahita reads the note, "I'll be back for you. Blaze." Anahita says, "but I thought Elliot and Blaze were both dead!." Josh says, "Blaze's a fire Elemental.. the flames must've healed him." Matteo says, "so he escaped and left behind a note for Anahita? We have to get you out of her...now!." Aztec says, "Matteo's right, Anahita. The water Elemental is the most powerful of all Elementals, if you die, all four Elementals will be wiped *out. FOREVER!.*" Anahita asks, "*am I in danger of dying? Damn, I'm really that important huh?.*" Aztec says, "*believe it or not...yes. you're now the most important person in our world, every Elemental will want to enslave you... and those who fear Elementals will want you dead.*" Matteo says, "*then we'll hide out at our family estate.*" Aztec says, "*that's a dangerous idea, son. an Elemental or a Hunter won't care if you're standing in their way... they will try to kill you, too. You shouldn't involve the family in Anahita's Elemental issues.*" Anahita says, "*maybe you're right sir.. I don't want anyone to be in danger because of me but Matteo is old enough to make his own decisions.*"

Chapter 11

Matteo says, *"yes I can, and I'll take any risk for you, Anahita."* Aztec says, *"fine, but I'm staying here to guard the academy. Good luck dealing with Sierra."* Aztec says, *"Josh, let's go."* Anahita asks, *"who's Sierra?."* Matteo replies, *"my mother Sierra rules our family with an iron fist.. she won't accept anything less than perfection.. then there's my cousin Araceli always thinks he'll find happiness at the bottom of a bottle and my two sisters, Lucy, and Shannon.. Lucy's an angel but Shannon she's a menace. We've always been more like competitors than siblings. My parents raised us to believe that Elementals are dangerous and unpredictable, but they know I trust you so if you can impress them.... they will have no choice but to accept you as my mate."* Anahita asks, *"what if they don't like me?."* Matteo replies, *"I know how to make sure that they do. Anahita it's so important to me that my family accepts you, this outfit will kick things off on the right foot."* He shows her a few options as she chooses a sweet dress; they soon drive off and reach a big mansion; Sierra says, *"ah my boy is home!."* Sierra and Matteo share a hug as he says, *"I missed you too mom!."* Sierra looks at Anahita saying, *"you must be the Elemental."* Matteo says, *"this is Anahita, she's not just an Elemental.. she's my mate."* Sierra is surprised while Araceli and Lucy come out; Araceli says, *"wow... our Alpha has finally found his mate."* Sierra says, *"and you..."* As Sierra looks over Anahita, her face has a worried expression wondering, *'does she not approve of me?.'* However, Sierra says, *"you are very quiet, dear."* Araceli says, *"yes, I'd expect an Alpha's mate to show more confidence."* Sierra says, *"especially when that mate is supposedly a powerful Elemental.. I'm sorry, Anahita but you're no match for my son."* Anahita looked stunned saying, *"I am, you're just underestimating me! I'm nervous too."* Sierra says, *"you've given me no reason to."* Matteo says, *"mom you've barely given her a chance!."* Araceli says, *"Anahita, you will be protected here."* Sierra says, *"but only because you're in grave danger and my son refuses to leave your side, I still don't find you worthy of being his mate."* Anahita sighs asking, *"what can I do to change your mind?."* Sierra replies, *"there is one thing...."* Sierra brings Matteo and Anahita to another room with two glasses and a bottle of liquid; Sierra says, *"here it is, Philia Mead, when Matteo's father and I became mates, we drank this together... it holds powers of love and protection, it will show you your dreams for the future...."* Matteo says, *"and help them come true, Anahita. I've always dreamed of drinking this with my mate someday."* Sierra says, *"this will show me that you're serious about being Matteo's mate."* Anahita feels Matteo's family has their doubts as she says, *"I'll do it."* Sierra pours two glasses as Matteo says, *"I love you Anahita."* Anahita says, *"I love you too Matteo."* They both drink as they look into each other's eyes and sees memories of them together as Wolves and also a little family. Anahita smiles at Matteo who smiles back lovingly. Sierra says, *"you have proven be my son's mate! Welcome to the family!."* Sierra hugs Anahita before inviting her for dinner; soon after dinner Matteo is about to tell Anahita something however Sierra says, *"Matteo, please show Anahita to the guest bedroom, you're still under my roof."* Matteo nods saying, *"of course mom."* Later in the bedroom Anahita finishes her facial as there is a knock on the door; Anahita opens to see Matteo as he says, *"I want to show you something..."* He takes her hand and brings her to his room as she looks around saying, *"so this is Alpha Matteo's childhood bedroom."* Matteo says, *"hot, right?."* Anahita says, *"I thought we were supposed to stay in separate bedrooms?."* Matteo replies, *"we could... unless you feel like breaking the rules."* He winks at her playfully as she blushes saying, *"I always feel like breaking the rules, what did you have in mind?."* Matteo says, *"good to know, spend the night with me here in my room, Anahita."* Matteo comes closer as his eyes darken and his voice low and husky. Matteo whispers, *'no one ever has to know....'* Anahita says, *"ok."* Matteo smiles as he kisses her before carrying her to the bed where they soon get intimate; later that night Anahita is sleeping cuddled in Matteo's arm when they suddenly wake up to a crash noise. Anahita asks, *"what was that?."* Matteo replies, *"don't worry you're going to be ok! I won't let anyone hurt you."* Matteo gets up and says, *"I'm going to check it out!."* Anahita says, *"I'm coming with you."*

Chapter 12

Matteo says, *"you need to stay here, Anahita"*. Anahita says, *"I'm not going to let you face any danger alone!"*. Matteo sighs saying, *"ok stay behind me Anahita, I won't let anyone, or anything hurt you"*. They head downstairs as Anahita says, *"it's pitch dark, I can't see anything..."* however just then they both hear a creak sound as Matteo starts fighting; Anahita says, *"MATTEO!"*. Anahita hears the muffled sounds of a tussle then Matteo's voice breaks through the darkness. Matteo says, *"Anahita, hit the lights!"*. Anahita hits the light. Anahita sees a young woman who smiles saying, *"hello brother, so nice to see you"*. Matteo says, *"Shannon, I should have known"*. Shannon sees Anahita asking, *"is this the 'Elemental mate' mom was worrying about? she's a funny weird adorable kind of thing isn't she?"*. Anahita comes over annoyed saying, *"you can't talk about me like that? guess the toxic jealousy jumped out!"*. Matteo says, *"Anahita's right unless you want me to choke you again. Anahita's the most powerful Wolf in our world right now... you should watch how you speak to her"*. Shannon says, *"you want to know what I think? No damn girl is worth putting all of our asses on the line! Mate or not!"*. Matteo says, *"it's your duty as part of this family to protect her, sis!"*. Shannon rolls her eyes asking, *"or what? she'll soak me to death?"*. Anahita replies, *"actually, that's not a bad idea"*. Anahita feels her own anger swell into a surge of power tingling just beneath her skin; she conjures a blue energy ball and aims it at Shannon who

is soon soaked; she cough as Anahita says, *"look who's boss now!"*.
Matteo asks, *"are you done, sis? Have you learned your lesson?"*.
Shannon is about to reply just as Sierra comes out asking, *"what's
with all the commotion? Why are you soaked, Shannon?"*.
Shannon glares at Anahita as Matteo says, *"mom don't worry
about it! you go back to bed"*. Sierra leaves as Shannon says,
"tomorrow I'm coming for your title, bro". Anahita looks at Matteo
asking, *"what's she talking about? what title?"*. Matteo replies,
*"the annual family baseball game... I've won and beaten everyone
every year since I started walking"*. Shannon says, *"until this year..."*.
Matteo says, *"we'll see who comes out on top, sis!"*. Shannon leaves
as Matteo brings Anahita back to their room to sleep. The next
morning Anahita is doing yoga and stretches as Matteo comes
in with a tray of breakfast; Anahita says, *"go, Shannon makes
Elliot look like a saint"*. Matteo says, *"yeah, she resents me for
being our parent's favourite and for finding my mate first, I'm
sure"*. Anahita drinks some juice and eats the toast before asking,
"let's make sure to teach her a lesson today". Matteo says, *"I think
she's an idiot which is even worse sometimes that's why we've got
to roast her at this baseball game today... knock her ego down a
peg"*. Anahita giggles as Matteo feeds her a strawberry covered
chocolate just as her phone beeps; Anahita sees the reminder as
Matteo asks, *"what's up Anahita?"*. Anahita replies, *"there's been
so much going on, I almost forgot my 18th birthday.... which is
tomorrow"*. Matteo smiles saying, *"oh, I'm so happy you told me"*.
Anahita smiles saying, *"I hope we can make it special!"*. Matteo
kisses her saying, *"I'll make sure it is"*. He says, *"I actually got
something for you for the game... but it can also be an early birthday
present if you want"*. Anahita asks, *"what is it?"*. Matteo hands her
a bag as she opens to see matching shirts; Matteo says, *"no we'll*

match today and you'll be my good luck charm, Anahita". Anahita blushes and says, *"thanks, Matteo".* She heads into the bathroom and freshens up before wearing Matteo's shirt; she comes out as he extends his hand saying, *"let's go".* Soon at the field two group of cheerleaders cheer as Anahita asks, *"are you sure it's safe to be out here?".* Matteo replies, *"as long as we stay within the fences, we'll be safe".* Araceli says, *"plus if anyone's looking for you Anahita, this is the last thing they would expect you to be doing".* The game soon begins as Matteo is playing hard; Lucy says, *"Shannon is only up by one point... if Matteo scores, they'll be tied! If Shannon scores, it's over".* Shannon asks, *"how does it feel to losing, bro?".* Matteo replies, *"you tell me in a minute".* Anahita thinks, *'if Shannon catches that ball, it's all over for Matteo! I need to distract Shannon'.* Anahita says, *"hey Shannon!".* Shannon turns as Anahita asks, *"what do you think of this?".* Anahita does a little trick which keeps her distracted as she is not able to catch the ball. Lucy says, *"they are tied!".* Matteo runs over saying, *"we make a great team Anahita".* Shannon scowls watching them as she says, *"not for long bro...!".* She angrily punches Matteo in his stomach as Anahita screams, *"MATTEO!".*

Chapter 13

Anahita comes onto the field as Shannon says, *"oops...."* Araceli says, *"don't worry, Anahita, he'll heal quickly."* Shannon says, *"but the game's over, I win."* Araceli says, *"unless he has someone else take his turn...."* Shannon laughs saying, *"yeah like who? Lucy? Anahita?."* Matteo says, *"you're dead, Shannon!."* Matteo turns to Anahita as his face alight with determination; Matteo says, *"Anahita can do it."* Anahita says, *"yes I will do my best for you."* The game resumes as Anahita hits the ball high and does a full home run winning the game for Matteo. Matteo recovers and lifts Anahita in his arms happily saying, *"you won!."* Shannon gets annoyed and throws the ball over the fence as Araceli says, *"way to lose the ball, Shan!."* Shannon rolls her eyes saying, *"chill, I'll go get it."* Matteo says, *"forget it, it's too dangerous to cross the fence."* Shannon climbs as Matteo says, *"wait, Shannon-."* Shannon drops as the ball is thrown back submerged in flames. Anahita looks worried saying, *"Blaze?."* Anahita soon feels a strong smell of smoke hit her nose and begins to cough as Matteo says, *"everyone, back to the house, NOW!."* Everyone begins to run as Matteo takes Anahita's hand and they leave to get to the house however they are left shocked as it is engulfed in flames; Sierra cries saying, *"my house! My beautiful house!."* Shannon says, *"if we had been inside...."* Araceli says, *"there's no way we would have made it out."* Matteo says, *"looks like Blaze found us."* They soon head back to the academy as Matteo tells his dad everything that happened and says, *"Blaze burned down our entire estate... obviously he'll stop at nothing to get Anahita."* Aztec says, *"if Blaze takes control of Anahita's powers... he'll build an army and destroy us all. But we can take him on, we can win."* Shannon says, *"this is crap! We shouldn't have to sacrifice our lives for Anahita!."* Anahita gives her a cold look saying, *"then you can leave! I'm not forcing you to stay here."* Matteo says, *"you shouldn't have to, Blaze's more dangerous than any of you can imagine and Anahita is my mate. So, we all have to protect her."* Later that evening Matteo brings Anahita to a room saying, *"I don't want you staying in the dorms tonight."* Anahita looks around the room as Matteo says, *"I know it's not much, but we can spice it up... we'll turn this place into a birthday fantasy suite."* Anahita smiles as she closes her eyes just as Matteo decorates the room with candles and roses; Anahita soon opens her eyes saying, *"this is so romantic!."* She sees a red gift box on the table and opens it to find a sexy nightie; she changes as Matteo removes his shirt and says, *"no matter what happens I will never let you be in danger."* Anahita kisses Matteo hungrily as he responds back passionately; they soon begin to get intimate when suddenly the clock chimes; Matteo and Anahita look at the clock as Matteo says, *"it's officially midnight.. happy birthday Anahita!."* Anahita kisses Matteo passionately and they soon fall asleep; the next day everyone is busy with training as Anahita decides to call Neirah and lets her know what's been happening. Neirah says, *"bestie! Promise me you will stay safe!."* Anahita says, *"of course, besides, I am not alone! I have Matteo with me."* Neirah says, *"I knew you two would end up together."* Later that evening Anahita is in the room as Matteo says, *"come I have something to show you!."* He brings her to a room filled with presents, a banner which says, *'HAPPY BIRTHDAY!.'* Anahita says, *"oh my god! This is so amazing!."* Anahita heads back to the room and changes into a beautiful pink dress with heels; she comes out as Matteo says, *"wow... y-you look gorgeous!."* Anahita blushes saying, *"thanks Matteo!."* He turns off the light and brings out a five-tier cake with a candle and sparkler; the lights then turn back on as everyone claps as Vesta sings, *"happy birthday to you! happy birthday to you! happy birthday to Anahita! SURPRISE HAPPY BIRTHDAY ANAHITA!."* Matteo says, *"close your eyes and make a wish."* Anahita closes her eyes as she thinks, *'I wish for Matteo to love me forever and for us to escape all this danger.'* She opens her eyes and blows out the candle; Matteo says, *"everyone gather around, I have a special birthday gift for Anahita, the gift of my mark."* Everyone looks at Matteo as he says, *"Anahita you have my heart... now I want to give you my soul, I can't bear the thought of anyone else even thinking they can have you. I want everyone to know that you're mine and I'm yours."* Anahita smiles at Matteo saying, *"do it, Matteo. Mark me!."*

Chapter 14

Matteo smiles as he kisses Anahita; Matteo's mouth slowly travels down to Anahita's neck, leaving a trail of kisses behind; Anahita shudders as Matteo's hands grip her waist as he pulls her body against his. Suddenly his gentle kisses are replaced with the feeling of a sharp teeth breaking into her delicate neck; a sharp sensation of pain that quickly soon melts into intense pleasure... Matteo says, *"now you're all mine and you're so beautiful"*. Anahita says, *"this is the most incredible gift anyone's ever given me"*. Matteo says, *"you deserve it.. you deserve the world, Anahita"*. He comes closer and caresses her cheek softly as everyone cheers for them; Vesta says, *"oh my god... that's the most romantic thing I've ever seen"*. Scarlett scowls and then runs out in tears; Sierra says, *"a toast to Anahita and Alpha Matteo... our world's most beautiful and powerful couple"*. Everyone raises their glass as Araceli says, *"cheers!"*. A little while later; Matteo says, *"go ahead to sleep, birthday girl.. I'll tidy up here"*. Anahita kisses Matteo and leaves; she soon hears Aztec and Sierra in the corridor and hides behind the wall. Sierra says, *"Anahita is putting our whole family in danger. Blaze will capture her no matter what... how many of our children will have to die first?"*. Aztec says, *"you're right my love... Matteo won't survive this and without an Alpha, the academy will fall"*. Anahita thinks, *'I can't let Matteo and his family die for me... I'm sneaking out to handle Blaze myself'*. Anahita changes out of her party dress as Vesta is asleep however soon she wakes up and turns the light on making Anahita jump. Vesta asks, *"what are you doing, Anahita? It's late and you should be sleeping"*. Anahita replies, *"I'm going to sneak out... I'm protecting Matteo's family and using my powers for good... there's evil out there and I can fight it with good"*. Vesta says, *"you're so strong and brave, Anahita. Let's make sure you can sneak through the gates unseen!"*. Vesta opens her wardrobe and hands Anahita an outfit saying, *"here, wear this!"*. Anahita gets change as Vesta says, *"now that's more like it"*. Anahita says, *"I don't feel comfortable! I feel like a catwoman!"*. Vesta says, *"in the dark, you'll practically be invisible in this outfit"*. Anahita gets changed as Vesta opens her window and helps Anahita to climb down; she sneaks out the back however soon sees Araceli with a crossbow by the gate. Araceli says, *"hey!!! you can't be out here! I'm calling for backup..."*. Anahita says pleadingly, *"NO! please"*. Araceli calls out, *"JOSH!!!"*. Anahita thinks, *'please forgive me for this'.* She comes to Araceli and punches him a few times until he falls before Anahita goes; she says, *"I'm so sorry to have to do this"*. Anahita runs as Araceli soon gets up saying, *"you'll be punished for this!"*. Anahita runs down into the forest as she suddenly sees a soft glow through the trees; suddenly the ground starts shaking and she feels herself fly backwards; an unknown figure stands in the shadow as Anahita asks, *"who are you? stay away from me! I'll fight you!"*. She is about to attack when Ajax turns to her saying, *"I am not here to hurt you, Anahita. I'm the Earth Elemental and we're all in danger... Blaze has been hunting me too... he wants to build an Elemental army and rule over all Wolves... the academy will be his castle.. the students will do his offering... and he requires your power to do it"*. Anahita asks, *"what about Matteo?"*. Ajax replies, *"Blaze will kill him, of course"*. Anahita asks, *"why should I trust you? how do I know this is not a trap?".* Ajax replies, *"because Anahita I know you better that you think and I would never hurt you... you see, I'm-".* Just then a fireball hits Ajax sending him against the wall; Anahita says, *"NO!".* Anahita feels a rough hand grab her from behind, and a warm unpleasant breath on her neck. Blaze says, *"sounds like old man's got it all figure out but he left out one very vital piece of my plan... you know how I'm going to create my Elemental army, Anahita?".* Anahita turns and freezes in fear asking, *"w-what? w-what are you going to do?".* Blaze replies, *"I'm going to mate with you.. with our combined powers, we can force any Wolves in the world to join our ranks".* Blaze yanks Anahita's arm back sending a wave of pain through her body. She feels his hot, reeking breath on her neck as he whispers in her ears *"and we'll create the most POWERFUL children in the world".* Back at the academy Matteo was made informed of Anahita's escape and said, *"I'm going to look for her".* Sierra says, *"son you need stay here! it's not safe out there".* Matteo says, *"mom, I'll be fine... she's my mate".*

Chapter 15

Back in the forest Blaze was taunting and gloating in Anahita's ears as she says, *"no way in hell, I'm letting that happen!."* Anahita bites his hand and headbutts Blaze before running; Blaze angrily says, *"OWW, what the fuck?!."* Anahita is running until she sees a familiar face; Matteo says, *"Anahita!."* Anahita says, *"Matteo!."* Blaze comes behind them as he says, *"you're wasting your energy, Matteo, she won't be your mate for much longer."* Ajax comes in front of them saying, *"you take Anahita, I can manage him Matteo!."* Anahita says, *"we can trust, Matteo... he's the Earth Elemental and he didn't hurt me."* Matteo says, *"fine.. then let's go."* They transform into their wolf form and run as Ajax and Blaze have a little fight; soon in a corner Matteo and Anahita transform back into their human form as Matteo says, *"what the hell do you think you're doing Anahita?! Running off to face Blaze without me?!."* Anahita replies *"I was protecting you, Matteo!."* Matteo says, *"I don't need protecting! You're my mate, Anahita and you betrayed me. we are supposed to be in this together and instead you're running off on dangerous missions alone...."* Anahita says, *"Matteo I promise I was looking out for us..."* He holds her as he says, *"I don't want to hear that."* Anahita feels his fiery gaze burn a hole into her soul; he takes a deep breath saying, *"I want you to tell me why you did it, the whole truth."* Anahita takes a deep breath replying, *"after the party I was on my way to bed when I overheard your parents talking... they told me that me being with you was putting everyone in danger... I could never bear the thought of anything happening to you... I wanted to keep you safe and everyone else."* Anahita feels tears forming in her eyes as Matteo takes his hand and caresses her cheek saying, *"I'm sorry Anahita, I had no idea.. you need to trust me when I say that no matter what I will always be there for you and protect you... you're my mate! I will never let anyone break us apart... I love you."* Anahita says, *"you're mine too! I will never leave your side... I love you too!."* They are about to kiss when Blaze comes there angrily saying, *"you're rejecting your true nature, Anahita."* Anahita and Matteo both look at Blaze angrily as Anahita says, *"what do you mean? I'm not like you! you don't even know me!."* Blaze says, *"you're more like me than you think, you'll never find happiness mating with someone else, Anahita... Elementals are born to be evil, to be all powerful... give into you true nature and become my mate instead."* Anahita comes in front and shields Matteo says, *"NEVER! I LOVE MATTEO! He's my only mate."* Blaze was about to throw a fireball at Matteo saying, *"I know what I can do, capture and enslave Anahita... and then I'll kill you Matteo!."* Matteo says, *"if you want to take her... then you'll have to go through me first."* Anahita says, *"no back up Matteo, I've got this!."* Matteo turns to Anahita says, *"but Anahita-."* Anahita takes a deep breath saying, *"I can deal with him, Matteo!."* Blaze laughs coldly saying, *"do you really think you can stop my plan, Anahita? You've had your powers for all of two seconds whereas I've been training harnessing mine for a lifetime."* Matteo holds her hand and says, *"Anahita, think of our bond! Use it to give you strength... use it to give you power."* Blaze holds a fireball saying, *"shut up! if you won't surrender to me, Anahita... then I will make you."* Anahita closes her eyes as she thinks of Matteo and soon uses her power to create a water soaking which pushes Blaze aside. Blaze gets up saying, *"you're only buying yourself useless time!."* Ajax comes there saying, *"I wouldn't call it useless!."* Ajax uses his powers to create an earthquake as Anahita feels the ground shaking; Matteo says, *"I've got you, Anahita!."* Blaze says, *"what the hell?! Make this stop!."* Ajax says, *"you're not our ruler, Blaze!."* Blaze says, *"we'll see about that."* Matteo says, *"Ajax, stop!."* Ajax says, *"no! I cannot let him use his power!."* Anahita's eyes darken as she steps forward and uses her power saying angrily, *"THIS IS FOR TRYING TO KILL MY MATE!."* Anahita's hand finds Blaze's throat as she feels all the tingling power beneath her skin race to her fingertips; as Blaze's eyes widen and he screams out in pain, Anahita grips him tighter power still surging through her body in waves. Blaze calls out weakly, *"st-s-st-stop...."* Matteo says stunned, *"Anahita, what are you-?."* Anahita feels the glow and power getting stronger replying, *"I don't know Matteo, I can't stop it!."* Matteo says, *"focus on my voice! Let him go!."* Anahita closes her eyes for a moment and lets Blaze go as he coughs out bright red blood. Blaze soon drops the floor as Matteo and Ajax looked on shocked; Matteo says, *"Anahita, you killed him."*

Chapter 16

Anahita was stunned by Blaze's body as Matteo and Ajax looked at her. Aztec soon arrived with Josh and Araceli who were both shocked seeing Blaze's dead body; Aztec says, *"she didn't just kill him... she bled him dry... Anahita, who ARE you?"*. Anahita replies, *"I-I couldn't control it, I couldn't fight nor stop it!"*. Aztec says, *"I told you, Matteo... her power is dangerous"*. Anahita says, *"Blaze was going to kill us! I used my power because I had to"*. Matteo says, *"I know and I'm glad to be alive right now"*. Aztec says, *"that's not the point, she could have-"*. Anahita suddenly sees an arrow flies out of the trees heading straight for her however Matteo pushes her aside and takes the hit on his chest; Anahita says, *"MATTEO!!"*. Everyone gathers around him as he says, *"go, follow them"*. Anahita says, *"you're hurt Matteo! how can I leave you?"*. Matteo replies, *"be careful... I don't want you getting hit too"*. He closes his eyes as Anahita kisses him saying, *"I've got this under control, and I'll do my best!"*. She gets up as Josh says, *"I'll watch over him, Anahita"*. Anahita runs off into the other part of the wood and soon sees the unknown person hiding behind the tree; she says, *"I see you!"*. The unknown person fires another arrow as Anahita uses her power to block the arrow; the person comes out from behind the tree saying, *"you're tough, Anahita... but your days are numbered"*. Anahita asks, *"who are you?! what do you want?!"*. The person replies, *"my name is Selene and I'm here to hunt you and all dangerous Wolves... you see I'm one of* many, your reckless magic attracted my attention.. you nearly flooded the grounds of this academy.... you instigated war against Beta Elliot, you drained the blood from a man's body". Anahita says, "you don't understand, I was defending myself-". Selene says, "your power has disrupted the natural order of our world. now you must be killed, once I alert the other Hunters... there will be no more elementals". Selene is about to fire another arrow as Anahita turns to run away; Selene says, "if you can't face me, then good luck fighting off Luke.. he's by far the most dangerous Hunter.. guns are his weapons of choice, and he won't hesitate to shoot". Soon at the academy Sierra was by Matteo's side as he lays on the bed. Aztec says, "it was only a matter of time until the Hunters came, the arrow that hit Matteo was poisoned with Wolfsbane". Anahita looks at Josh saying, "I can't bear to see him suffer! Is there an antidote?!". Aztec replies, "the poison has to run its course, he'll be in extreme pain as long as it's in his blood". Ajax says, "there could be another antidote, you were able to drain Blaze's blood, Anahita... you could use your power to suck out the poison from Matteo's blood too...". Aztec says, "she drained Blaze's blood because she was out of control! She's going to kill my son! her own mate!". Shannon says, "dad's right! I may not have seen what she did, but I don't want her endangering Matteo's life!". Matteo's face twists in agony as another wave of intense pain washes over him. Matteo says pleadingly, "Anahita, please.... help me". Anahita takes a deep breath as she kisses Matteo; a light golden glows around them as Matteo soon feels his pain going. Anahita soon breaks the kiss as Matteo closes his eyes. Sierra says, "Matteo! My baby boy!". She looks at Anahita asking, "what have you done? have you killed him?". Anahita looks worried as Josh checks Matteo's pulse saying, "he's asleep..". Ajax examines him saying, "the poison has *been successfully removed"*. As everyone gathers around Matteo waiting for him to wake up; Ajax asks, *"Anahita, can I speak with you for a moment?"*. They head out as Ajax says, *"we need to warn the other Elementals about the Hunters, if we can bring them all here... the Hunters won't stand a chance of taking us down... we'll start by finding the new Fire Elemental"*. Anahita says, *"new Fire Elemental?"*. Ajax nods replying, *"when you killed Blaze, his power was passed down to a descendant"*. Anahita asks, *"do you know who it is?"*. Ajax replies, *"I have a pretty good idea, Blaze's place is a cabin in the woods which have rogue guards everywhere... they won't let anyone near the next Elemental"*. Anahita asks, *"why so many guards?"*. Ajax replies, *"to keep you out of course... so ready to take a little trip tomorrow?"*. Anahita nods saying, *"I'll meet you in the morning"*. Anahita soon heads to bed; the next morning she comes to check on Matteo who is feeling better and is having soup. Anahita asks, *"how are you feeling, Matteo?"*. Matteo replies, *"better thanks to you!"*. He smiles at her as she tells him about the trip. Anahita says, *"this is a dangerous trip to take..."*. Matteo gets up saying, *"I can't let you go alone... I don't trust Ajax!"*. Anahita shares her doubts however says, *"he's been an Elemental a lot longer than I have"*.

Chapter 17

Matteo says, *"which means he could use his knowledge against you, Anahita. We need to stay one step ahead of him"*. Anahita looks at Matteo deep in his eyes as his expression is clouded with worry. Anahita says, *"you know we will"*. They soon freshen up and head out as Ajax is in the car saying, *"ready for an adventure?"*. They nod and come in as Ajax asks, *"oh Matteo, could you make sure my weapon bag is in the trunk?"*. Matteo replies, *"sure...."*. He comes out and is about to open the trunk as Ajax drives off; Anahita says, *"we can't just leave Matteo behind!"*. Ajax says, *"where we are going, Matteo can't follow nor come"*. Anahita says annoyed, *"what the hell are you talking about?!"*. Ajax replies, *"my name is Ajax and I'm your father, Anahita. I'm taking you home!"*. Anahita felt angry saying, *"you can't control me! you're lying too!"*. Ajax replies, *"it's the truth! Did you really think I would let you walk into a literal death trap? I'm doing what's best for you"*. Anahita says, *"then I'm getting out of here!"*. Suddenly Anahita hears screeching tires and sees a flash of Matteo's sports car; Ajax says, *"he really does not give up...."*. Anahita opens the window and screams, *"MATTEO!!!! HEELP!"*. Ajax says, *"calm down!"*. Anahita turns her eyes back to the road, she notices something straight ahead... Anahita says, *"there's a rock ahead! It's blocking Matteo's path! He's going too fast... if we don't swerve, he'll hit it!"*. Ajax says, *"not my problem!"*. Anahita hears the squealing of breaks as Matteo tries to slow down; Anahita grabs the wheel and swerves as Ajax stops the car; she comes out and runs to Matteo who comes out of his car asking, *"Anahita, are you ok?"*. Anahita looks at Ajax asking, *"are you mad? you almost killed Matteo!"*. Ajax says, *"this is between me and my daughter! you don't need to get involved Matteo!"*. Matteo angrily says, *"get the fuck out of here! I won't let you take Anahita away from me!"*. Anahita takes Matteo's hand saying, *"I'm not leaving him!"*. Ajax says, *"fine, I wanted to keep Anahita safe, but I guess it's up to you then...."*. Ajax gets back in his car and drives off as Matteo says, *"he's making a big mistake, Anahita.... I will never leave you like that!"*. Anahita kisses Matteo saying, *"neither will I.. are you sure you're ok? you're not hurt!"*. Matteo says, *"I'm fine, I know this place we can rest..."* They head into the woods as night begins to fall; Matteo says, *"these woods are legendary, and this waterfall is special..."*. Anahita sees the fireflies and water asking, *"what's so special about this waterfall?"*. Matteo replies, *"it's called the waterfall of soulmates, if you come here on a full moon with a pure heart and wish for your perfect mate, this magic water will grant your wish"*. Anahita smiles saying, *"this is so romantic, have you made a wish here?"*. Matteo replies, *"as a matter of fact, I have. The last time I was here I wished for you"*. Anahita kisses Matteo who responds back warmly and passionately; Anahita says, *"you know it's a full moon again tonight..."*. Matteo says, *"I know what I wish for..."*. Anahita asks, *"what is your wish, Matteo?"*. Matteo replies, *"we have a battle to fight, Anahita and right now it feels like the whole world is against us but all I wish for right now is you, All of you!"*. Anahita feels his body burning with desire as she sees Matteo's eyes longing for her; Matteo takes her hand and brings her behind the waterfall to a cave saying, *"I want to take you right her and make you mine... and finally unite our bodies the way we've united our souls here in the waterfall of soulmates".* Anahita pulls Matteo's closer as he kisses her passionately and then begins to remove her clothes as she does the same their kiss and touch becomes more intimate; Anahita moans Matteo's name as Matteo says, *"I love when you moan my name like that!".* Anahita tickles Matteo playfully as he pins her gently to the wall and kisses her neck; A few hours later Anahita rests in Matteo's arm as their hands are held together. He kisses her forehead as Anahita looks at Matteo saying, *"we should get going, without my dad here, it's just me against the Hunters".* Anahita grabs her clothes and changes as Matteo does the same saying, *"it's never just you, Anahita, we're in this together and we'll go to Blaze's cabin together".* They soon come out as Matteo extends his hand to Anahita who holds it as he says, *"we'll find that fire Elemental before the Hunters do".* They soon make their way further into the forest before spotting the cabin.

Chapter 18

Anahita asks, *"you think we can make a run for it, Matteo?"*. Matteo replies, *"if we make it past that guard, we can get through the door and whatever waits for us inside... we'll deal with it together"*. Matteo takes Anahita's hand as they prepare to run out of the woods; A rogue says, *"hey you!"*. The rogue rushes towards Anahita with a knife in his hand; Anahita kicks him as he stumbles on the ground; Matteo says, *"nice kick, Anahita!"*. They are about to head to the door when suddenly Anahita is shot as she feels the pain in her leg; another rogue holding a knife says, *"I got you!"*. Anahita looks down at the wound as the bright red blood pours from the bullet wound; Anahita feels her vision getting weaker as the blinding pain takes over her senses; she collapses as her eyes slowly begin to close as Matteo calls out, *"ANAHITA!"*. A few moment later Anahita wakes up as she says, *"what the-"*. She tries to sit up, but something is holding her back; Matteo is next to her on the bed saying, *"Anahita, we're both tied up, someone snuck up on us! I don't know what they are planning... but we have to get out of here!"*. Anahita tries to use her power and lift her hands however she can barely move. Anahita says, *"it's not working, my hands are tied too tightly"*. A voice says, *"stop fighting! It's useless!"*. An angry voice calls from the other side of the door as Anahita notices a smoke curling up asking, *"who are you?! show yourself!"*. Vesta reveals herself saying, *"it's me, your roomie!"*. Matteo says, *"Vesta?!"*. Anahita asks, *"you're the next fire*

Elemental?!". Vesta holds a fireball in her hand replying, *"surprise! Blaze's my uncle.. that night of your birthday when I helped you sneak out... I was leading you straight into Blaze's trap but then you killed him, so now it's my turn to kill Matteo!"*. Anahita says, *"no, Vesta! Blaze was evil! He wanted to hurt and enslave innocent people!"*. Vesta says, *"you just didn't understand his vision... you always did seem cool Anahita, so I'll give you two time to say your goodbyes"*. She throws the fireball on the floor which soon start growing around them. Vesta says, *"you don't have much time though!"*. Anahita says, *"no, you don't have to do this!"*. Matteo says, *"it's ok, Anahita, if we don't make it out of this just know that I love you and if you really love me too then we will find each other in the next life"*. Anahita brings her head closer to Matteo saying, *"I love you Matteo and I will never stop loving you!"*. Vesta says, *"aww poor lovebirds! your hope is running out..."*. Just as she is about throw another fireball there is a gust of wind which knocks her out; Araceli stops the fire and opens the rope for Matteo and Anahita. Araceli says, *"Anahita, your leg"*. Anahita says, *"I was shot by a rogue"*. Araceli says, *"here, let me help"*. Anahita sits as Araceli closes his eyes as he holds his hands over her leg, suddenly she feels a twinge of pain as the bullet rises out from the already healing wound. Matteo says, *"Araceli? you're..."* Araceli replies, *"the air Elemental? yeah I meant to tell you about that"*. Anahita asks, *"how did you find us?"*. Araceli replies, *"I followed you in case you needed my help, I felt guilty standing by while you were fighting to protect us"*. Anahita says, *"thank you Araceli"*. Matteo says, *"yes, you saved my life, cuz"*. Araceli says, *"I took out the rest of the rogues outside with a little tornado so we should be good to go"*. Suddenly an arrow flies in as he screams, *"everyone get down!"*. Vesta wakes up asking, "wh-what's going on?". Anahita says, *"I thought you said you took care of all the rogues, Araceli?"*. Araceli holds the arrow saying, *"it's poisoned! These aren't rogues... the Hunters have found us"*. They all get up and head towards the back exit as Vesta begs, *"please take me with you, I don't want the Hunters to get me"*. Anahita says, *"you almost killed me and Matteo!"*. Vesta says, *"but after Araceli knocked me out, it was like I woke up from a strange dream... I could totally kill you now if I wanted but I don't... we're friends! I promise I won't hurt any of you again"*. Anahita says, *"yeah, you won't because you're not as powerful as me"*. Matteo says, *"she's not kidding, Vesta"*. Araceli says, *"we don't have time for this! if we leave her here.... the Hunters could force her to use her power against us"*. Matteo searches Anahita's face with a blazing look in his eyes saying, *"Anahita, we need to be the ones who control her power... we need to take her with us"*. Anahita says, *"sorry Matteo, I'm not taking any chances... we leave her behind"*. Vesta says, *"no, no, PLEASE!"*. They leave as Vesta sighs sadly; soon outside they are cornered by the Hunters as Araceli says, *"let's kick some Hunter asses!"*.

Chapter 19

Matteo says, *"let's do this!"*. Araceli and Anahita use their power as Matteo kicks and fights the rest. Anahita soon sees another Hunter approaching as she distracts him, and Matteo beats him. Matteo says, *"see if any of these guys mess with us again-"*. Araceli says, *"Matteo look out!"*. Anahita sees a guy holding a gun at Matteo; she says, *"I know you... you're Luke aren't you?"*. Luke says, *"I see my reputation precedes me"*. Archaeli is about to strike however Luke says, *"don't even think about it, one step closer and he dies!"*. Matteo says, *"I'll be ok, Anahita"*. Luke says, *"I wouldn't be so sure about that"*. Anahita feels angry seeing Luke push the gun closer on Matteo's neck and attacks; Luke then grabs Matteo as Anahita says, *"please... just don't kill him"*. Luke says, *"that's all you have left to say? no self-sacrifice? I'm disappointed in you, Anahita"*. Anahita says, *"stop please"*. Luke says with an evil smirk, *"you really want him? then come to the academy and get him!"*. Luke grabs Matteo and runs off as Anahita is about to go after him just as Archaeli says, *"come I know something that will get us there faster"*. They both run down the path and head into Matteo's sports car. Araceli drives as Anahita says, *"if Luke's using Matteo as bait... then we have to get to the academy first"*. Araceli says, *"good thing Matteo's car goes faster than any Hunter can run, he'll be ok"*. Anahita says, *"this fight is between Hunters and Elementals. Matteo doesn't deserve this, and I could never forgive myself if anything happened to him...*

I couldn't go on". Araceli says, *"he'll be fine, and you will keep fighting until the end. The fate of every Elemental in this life and the lives to come are in your hands, Anahita. It's you who has the power to save them and yourself".* Suddenly the car jerks to a stop as smokes plummets from the hood; Araceli and Anahita both get out as Araceli says, *"DAMN!".* Anahita worries asking, *"what are we going to do now?".* Araceli replies, *"we transform into wolves and run like we've never run before".* Anahita nods and they both change into their wolf form and run; They sneak into the academy and slowly make their way to the rooftop as they see Matteo tied up with his family surrounded by Hunters. Araceli says, *"we need to get them out of there".* Anahita says, *"I'll attack Luke, you untie the others".* Araceli asks, *"how will you attack, Anahita?".* Anahita replies, *"I'll sneak attack from behind! I will use my power".* Araceli says, *"Luke's got nothing on you".* Anahita says, *"let's do this!".* Araceli sneaks from another stairwell as Anahita comes behind and uses his waterpower to sneak up on the Hunters who fall one by one. Araceli frees everyone as they come over to Anahita's side; Luke says, *"you two think you are so smart, aren't you? always finding your way back together".* Matteo takes Anahita's hand; Anahita says, *"you wish you had what we have, that's why me and Matteo are mates".* Matteo says, *"It's actually impossible to keep us apart".* Luke says, *"oh wait... I almost forgot".* The Hunters bring out Vesta as Luke says, *"she almost killed you once... I'm sure she can do it again".* Vesta uses her power and burns the Hunters as Luke turns shocked yelling, *"what the hell?".* Vesta runs over saying, *"actually I think I belong over here".* Anahita says, *"I think so too".* Luke says, *"so I guess you all have picked your sides, then. Now we have a real battle on our hands".* Matteo turns to Anahita taking his hand in yours;

he says, *"let's end this right here, with me by your side Anahita... your power is strong enough to stop this war before it even starts".* He caresses her cheek saying, *"kiss me, take my love for you and turn it into power".* Anahita kisses Matteo as a bright golden glow engulfs around them. Suddenly Anahita's eyes deepen as she says, *"this is enough! We will not fight!".* Luke says angrily, *"what are you going to do? kill me? like you killed Elliot and his friend? are you going to drain the life out of me, too?".* Anahita replies, *"I told you, that is NOT who I am".* Luke gets on his knees saying, *"really? Show me?".* Matteo says, *"you've got this, Anahita. I believe in you.. show everyone that you can control your power and you are good".* Anahita uses her power and brings down the Hunters. Luke looks stunned as Anahita soon says, *"enough with the war!".* Luke grab his gun and points it at Matteo as Anahita says, *"NO!".* Suddenly Araceli leaps forward throwing his arms out to send a gust of wind straight at Luke however Luke shoots twice; everyone is stunned and shocked as Anahita screams, *"ARCAELI!".* Matteo holds Araceli in his arm as Luke fixes his gaze on Anahita saying, *"I guess dying is really not your destiny, Anahita".* Anahita says, *"no, so you might as well stop trying".* Luke says, *"but... I can't just let you go".* Anahita says, *"you can because I'm not the villain you think I am, and otherwise more innocent people will get hurt and this war will never end.. you think my family will stop fighting after I'm gone? you might win this battle, but you will never win the war".*

Chapter 20

Luke says, *"you know... you actually might be right, it's clear to me now that you want to use your power for good... that all of you Elementals do so I will leave you now, but I will be keeping an eye on you, Anahita".* Luke leaves with his Hunters as Anahita turns to Matteo who's face is screwed up with anguish; Anahita glances around at everyone who is all shadowed with sadness. Anahita asks, *"he's going to be ok, right?".* Matteo replies, *"Anahita, the bullet hit his heart... I don't think he'll survive".* Vesta bends down to Araceli while Anahita says, *"there must be something we can do".* Sierra says, *"we never even got to know him as his true self.. we never got to tell him we accept him for who he really is".* Anahita says, *"I'm not giving up on him. there has to be more we can do".* Aztec says, *"I think there could be, Araceli is an Elemental, you and Vesta are both Elementals not to mention your power is stronger than ever".* Vesta says, *"yeah, think of what we could do if the two of us combine our power".* Ajax says, *"make that that the three of us".* Anahita looked angrily at Ajax asking, *"what the hell are you doing here? trying to kidnap me again?".* Ajax replies, *"I was a coward before, but this should have been my fight too, if I can help now, then I want to."* Matteo says, *"I know it's hard to trust him, god knows it is for me... but this might be our only chance to save Araceli".* Lucy says, *"please Anahita, will you save him?".* Anahita nods saying, *"yes, we'll do everything we can".* Vesta asks, *"so how do we do this?".* Anahita says, *"take my hand, channel your power into me while you imagine healing him".* Ajax and Vesta hold Anahita's hand while everyone watches; Shannon asks, *"is this supposed to be happening?".* Matteo replies, *"let Anahita handle it".* All three of them close their eyes as a glow forms around them before touching Araceli. Matteo says, *"it's working";* A burst of light shines from Anahita's chest into Araceli as she says, *"now let go of my hand".* Vesta asks, *"did it work?".* Araceli's wound disappear as he opens his eyes; Araceli asks, *"w-what happened?".* Anahita smiles excitedly as Matteo comes over saying, *"oh my god, Anahita you did it!".* Anahita says, *"we all did it! you believed in me Matteo!".* Araceli gets up and thanks Anahita as he hugs her happily. Araceli sees everyone and hugs them as Anahita feels dizzy; Sierra says, *"finally... our whole family is together and safe... all thanks to Anahita".* Anahita feels her vision getting blurry as she says, *"m-Matteo?".* Anahita falls as Ajax holds her saying, *"Anahita!".* Matteo comes over and carries her to his room as they call the doctor. The doctor examines Anahita as Matteo asks, *"what's wrong with her doctor?".* The doctor smiles replying, *"she's pregnant!".* Matteo and the family are excited as Anahita opens her eyes; Matteo kisses her saying, *"I'm going to be a dad! you're going to be a mom".* He runs out for a moment before coming back with a small velvet box; he asks, *"Anahita, will you marry me?".* Anahita replies, *"A thousand times YES! I've never wanted anything more".* Matteo puts the ring on Anahita's finger as he kisses her warmly. Sierra says, *"a wedding?! How wonderful!!".* Shannon says, *"I know I've given you a lot of shit, Anahita but I'm happy for you two!".* Sierra says, *"this will be your official welcome into the family!".* A few weeks later Anahita is resting just as there is a knock on the door; Anahita says, *"come in".* Neirah says, *"hey bestie!".* Anahita looks on excited as she hugs Neirah happily saying, *"you look huge bestie!"*. Anahita says, *"I can't believe you're here!"*. Neirah says, *"I wouldn't miss my bestie's special day!"*. Vesta comes in with a tray of food and glass of orange juice. Anahita says, *"Vesta, this is my bestie Neirah!"*. Vesta says, *"it's nice to meet you Neirah"*. Anahita gets up saying, *"I need to stretch my legs!"*. Matteo soon comes and kisses her saying, *"how's my beautiful mate?"*. Anahita replies, *"I feel so big!"*. Anahita comes down as Sierra is busy with planning the baby shower; Anahita says, *"I forgot we have to head to the hospital to have the scan!"*. Sierra says, *"I have a feeling you will have a baby girl!"*. Aztec says, *"no she will have a boy!"*. They argue as Matteo takes Anahita's hand and kisses it saying, *"whatever it is, I don't mind as long as you are both healthy"*. Anahita blushes and they soon head to the hospital for the scan. As Anahita lays down the doctor comes and does the scan asking, *"are you ready to find out what you are having?"*. Matteo nods as the doctor replies, *"you're having.....twins! a boy and girl"*. Anahita says, *"twins?"*. Matteo kisses her happily. Anahita gets up as they head home to see the living room decorated; Sierra says, *"tell us! Did you find out what you're having? It's a girl right?"*. Aztec says, *"no way it's a boy!"*. Matteo says, *"actually it's both! A boy and girl!"*. Matteo says, *"I want to marry you tomorrow Anahita! make you mine before the babies are born"*. Anahita asks, *"how will I get ready for tomorrow?"*. Neirah and Vesta agree to help as Matteo heads with the guys to prepare; The next day in the afternoon Anahita was getting ready when she felt a little tingle in her stomach; She soon came downstairs and saw Ajax waiting for her. Ajax says, *"my baby girl is all grown up!"*. Anahita says, *"dad please..."*. Ajax extends his hand saying, *"come on, Matteo's waiting for you"*. They headed outside as Matteo smiled seeing Anahita in the white lace gown; she thinks smiling, *'my happy ever after...'*. Josh says, *"Matteo and Anahita are you ready to be wed?"*. Matteo extends his hand to Anahita who smiles at him as they both nod. Matteo says, *"Anahita, I vow to love you, to care for you, to respect you, to honour you and to stay by your side, now and always"*. Anahita says, *"Matteo, I vow to care for you, respect you, honour you and to cherish your now and always"*. Josh says, *"by the power vested in me... I now pronounce you officially Alpha and Elemental.. you may kiss your mate"*. Anahita and Matteo kiss as everyone cheers for them just as Anahita feels another tingle in her stomach and her water breaks. Matteo rushes her to the hospital as Anahita screams in pain; a few hours later the doctor says, *"congratulation your new babies!"*. Sierra holds the baby girl as Aztec holds the baby boy. Anahita extends her hand to Matteo who kisses her; Sierra hands Anahita her baby girl asking, *"what have you decided to name her?"*. Anahita replies, *"Alizeh"*. Ajax has tears in his eyes as Matteo holds his baby boy saying, *"his name will be Cassian"*. Neirah says, *"this moment requires a family picture"*. They all get together as the nurse comes in and takes the photo; Anahita thinks smiles, *'I got more than I expected today... Matteo finally my husband and our darling children'*. Matteo looks at Anahita thinking, *'I never expected that I would finally have Anahita as my Luna, my wife and the mother of my babies... all I want to forever is love her...'*. Anahita and Matteo share a kiss as everyone cuddles and holds Cassian and Alizeh.

CPSIA information can be obtained
at www.ICGtesting.com
Printed in the USA
BVHW052312261222
655035BV00009B/265